Tilly

FRANK E. PERETTI

Tilly

THE NOVEL

CROSSWAY BOOKS

A DIVISION OF
GOOD NEWS PUBLISHERS
WHEATON, ILLINOIS

Tilly

Original copyright © 1988 by Frank E. Peretti.

New edition, redesigned, copyright © 2003 by Frank E. Peretti.

Published by Crossway Books
    A division of Good News Publishers
    1300 Crescent Street
    Wheaton, Illinois 60187

Cover design: Kirk Dou Ponce
    UDG / DesignWorks, www.udgdesignworks.com

Cover photo: IMS Productions, filmmakers of the *Tilly* movie.

Printed in the United States of America

ISBN 0-7394-3684-8

To the original cast of "Tilly" . . .
an audiodrama, 1986

Foreword

Tilly is an extraordinary and unforgettable story that has touched the lives of so many—in a deep and lasting way.

Tilly is a beautifully written and remarkable story with a heart of truth that is undeniable. It tells the story of a young mother who made a regrettable decision earlier in her life—something that later came to haunt her deeply. But it tells the story especially of how she came to know the reality of God's forgiveness, and the recovery of joy and hope.

We are delighted to recommend *Tilly* to you—as a book that could change your life forever, as a story of hope for those in need of its message, and as a story to change the heart of America.

—Michael W. & Debbie Smith

One

It was a day in April. Spring had come again, just like always, laughing and teasing, full of comfort, the same old spring; it hadn't changed a bit. Light breezes, cool air left over from the stubbornly fading winter, played across the rolling turf of the old cemetery, carrying the scent of fruit blossoms, lilacs, and freshly mown grass. From somewhere beyond the orderly rows of gray and purple gravestones, birds chattered and sang with abandon.

April. Here it is again, Kathy thought. It surrounds this place. The world is filled with it. I should feel so warm right now.

But she felt cold, and fidgeted just a little as she stood there, her hand on Dan's arm, listening to Pastor Taylor's closing words.

"... inasmuch as God Almighty has taken unto Himself the soul of our departed brother, we commit the earthly house of his habitation back to the ground from which it came; earth to earth, ashes to ashes, dust to dust . . ."

Pastor Taylor was reading his words from a small book, but he was reading them slowly, digesting their meaning for himself before sharing them audibly.

". . . in the assurance that if the earthly house of our tabernacle be dissolved, we have a building of God, an house not made with hands, eternal in the heavens . . ."

It's so lonely out here, Kathy thought.

There were only three of them standing around that plain gray casket adorned with one simple flowered wreath. Their little graveside service was hardly noticeable, and Pastor Taylor's voice did not carry far.

"Let us pray," said Pastor Taylor.

They prayed the Lord's Prayer, just the three of them.

Pastor Taylor closed his little book and looked up. "That will end our interment service." Then he smiled, took a breath, and relaxed a little. "I want to thank you two for coming."

"Any time, Pastor Taylor," Dan replied.

"Glad to do it," said Kathy.

The minister looked down at the casket again. "Did you even know Frank Smith?"

Dan shook his head. "No, Pastor, not really. I used to buy the paper from him, and that's about it."

Pastor Taylor looked at them, and then scanned the surrounding cemetery. Dan and Kathy could feel it too, the great open distance that stretched so far on every side.

The minister said, "It really means a lot that you were here. Regardless of how well or how little we may have known him, it would have been a shame for Frank to pass away unmourned and unremembered."

"Well," said Kathy, "someone has to care, even if it's a stranger."

The pastor nodded and smiled. "Thank you for caring."

He meant it. Kathy felt warm for the first time.

"Thank you for a beautiful service," she said.

The cemetery's old caretaker stood by his truck some distance away. Pastor Taylor went to settle final arrangements with him, and Dan and Kathy started back across the cemetery toward their car.

"Yeah," Dan said quietly, "good old Frank Smith. Third and Amber won't be quite the same without him and that old newsstand."

"It was sad," said Kathy. "It was the smallest funeral I've ever been to."

"Well, that's just the way it goes. People get busy, they didn't know him, they have other things to do . . ."

"I wonder if they'll even miss him."

"I think they will. For a while anyway." They walked for a short distance more before Dan spoke his next thought. "He died alone, that's for sure. Guess they finally found him in his little hotel room . . ."

"No . . . That's enough."

Dan dropped the topic. He gave her a compliment. "I'm glad we came. It was a good idea."

She smiled and received his words, but had to say again, "It was sad."

"Yeah," he agreed. "It was." He groped for his car keys. "Tell you what. I could just bring the car around and pick you up over by the . . ."

Kathy squeezed his arm. She was looking across the cemetery. Dan quickly hushed.

Now he could see the woman too, young, dark, and very lovely, just beyond a row of aging monuments. She was kneeling in the grass, flowers in her hands, her head bowed in prayer. She was motionless, and the colors of her hair, the flowers, the grass were all so perfect. The picture brought them to a stop.

Kathy was awestruck. "Beautiful," she whispered. Dan nodded.

They watched. The woman stirred only enough to gently set the flowers on the grave.

"It makes you wonder what kind of story's behind it," Kathy said. "A husband gone before his time, or a son, or a brother lost in a war . . ." She smiled. "She's remembering."

Dan was a little shocked to feel Kathy moving in that direction. He held her back. "Hey . . . hey now . . ."

Kathy pulled from him. "Don't. I'm not going to do anything."

"Kathy, I'm sure this lady doesn't want any visitors right now."

Kathy was offended. "She won't have any. I just want to see the gravestone, that's all."

She pulled loose, and Dan didn't follow her. All he could do was watch and hope something terrible wouldn't happen.

Kathy stepped very lightly. She could hear the woman's muffled prayer, a soft, pleading supplication, mostly whispered, but sometimes sweetened by the clear, even tones of her voice. She seemed so lost in her prayer, so oblivious to her surroundings, that Kathy almost turned back, not wanting to shatter the moment. She decided just to be more careful.

She could just catch the corner of the stone over the woman's shoulder, but the glare of the sun washed out the inscription. Closer. Quiet. Just a little to one side. That's it.

Now she could see the name.

"Tilly."

It slipped out. The name struck her, touched her heart, and went to her lips before she could stop it. She didn't think anyone would hear such a faint whisper.

But the woman heard it. She gasped in surprise and looked up at Kathy, her dark eyes filled with dismay.

Kathy felt stabbed through with shame. "Oh . . . excuse me . . . please . . . I didn't mean to . . ."

But then the eyes widened. The woman turned away and looked only at the grave. She began to tremble.

"No . . ." Kathy fumbled, backing away. "No, don't . . . It's all right."

Oh! Kathy backed into Dan.

"Pardon us," he said with irritation in his voice. "We were just leaving."

The woman would not look at them. Now she had her hand to her face.

Kathy tried to be a friend. "Who . . . who was Tilly?"

The woman bolted like a frightened animal, scattering the flowers; she escaped, she ran desperately away, as if to save her life.

"No, wait!" Kathy cried. "We didn't mean any harm! Don't run!"

Dan's grip on Kathy's arm was almost painful. "Oh brother, I don't believe this!"

Kathy just couldn't seem to right this terrible wrong. "We're leaving, right now!" she called.

Dan spoke in a hushed voice, hoping she would take the hint. "Kathy, forget it. That's enough."

Kathy gave it up. The woman was gone. The day was ruined.

"I feel sick."

Dan had to force himself to be compassionate. "Well . . . Kathy, I was hoping you'd realize that this was one of those very private moments for her."

"I scared her, Dan. I scared her, and I didn't mean to."

"Oh . . ." Dan struggled to think of a reply that would soothe her. "It's . . . uh . . . emotions, you know. There are a lot of emotions at work in a place like this."

"Did you see the look on her face when she saw me?"

"Well . . . who knows what she was thinking? It's all emotions . . ."

Kathy looked at the little gravestone again. Now she could see it clearly. It bore just that one name: Tilly.

Tilly. She couldn't take her eyes away. She didn't want to. Somewhere else in the world, Dan was still talking, saying something about lunch, the car, the rest of the afternoon. But Kathy was looking at that stone.

Tilly. What date?

Kathy stooped down to look. Only one date. Only one. Nine years ago.

"Kathy . . ." came Dan's voice. Now she heard him. "What are you doing?"

Kathy didn't have an explanation, and she couldn't come up with one. "Tilly. I mean, that's all it says."

Dan could only say, "Hmm."

"And only one date. See here?"

Dan sighed and remained quiet for a moment. "I guess, like you were saying, there must be quite a story behind it. Is that what you're thinking?"

It was. "Oh . . . oh no, not really." She looked at the stone again. "It's just . . . It's . . . I don't know."

She could hear the jingle of his car keys.

"I'll go get the car. You can meet me out there by the—"

"I think I'll be here." Dan was quiet for an awkwardly long moment after that. She prodded him. "Just go ahead. I'll be here."

He didn't say another word. She could only hear his footsteps fading away.

Two

 $\mathcal{D}$ an rolled over and looked at the digital clock by the bed. One-thirty in the morning, and where was Kathy now? He didn't notice when she'd gotten up, but she was gone again, like so many nights before. He flopped onto his back and stared at the ceiling, his wrist on his brow. Should I get up and look for her? What if she snaps at me again? What if we get on each other's case again? Man, that just wouldn't be worth the trouble. Maybe I should just let it slide, let it pass, just try to keep the peace around here.

"Lord," he half-muttered and half-prayed, "we've got a real problem here, and I just don't know what to do."

He lay there thinking about it only for a short moment before he threw back the covers, swung his feet down to the floor and his waiting slippers, and grabbed his robe off a nearby chair.

The hallway outside the bedroom was dark, but

he could see a faint slit of light coming from under the door to his office. That had to be her.

He pushed the door open very slowly. Yes, there she was huddled on the small sofa in the light of the desk lamp, a large book cradled in her lap and fresh tears on her cheeks. She hadn't noticed him.

"Kathy?"

He startled her. She turned her head quickly away from him, frantically smearing the tears off her face.

"Are you all right?"

She seemed quite annoyed at the question. "Of course I'm all right."

Dan hesitated in the doorway. He kept thinking it might be better to just back out of this. "May I come in?"

She didn't answer. He finally took a chance and went in anyway, sitting very quietly, very carefully in his desk chair, not far from the sofa. Now he was facing her, and she couldn't turn away from him.

She wiped her face on the sleeve of her robe. "I wasn't crying."

Dan skipped that topic. He just looked at her for a very difficult, wordless moment. He noticed his fingers were drumming together. He held them still.

"Is there anything I can do?"

That was a safe thing to say. Kathy relaxed a little, and even wiped away another tear without hiding it.

"I don't know," was all she could say at first. Dan was afraid the conversation was over until she finally blurted, "I'm sorry, Dan, I really don't want to be this way."

"I know."

"You and the kids must think I'm terrible . . ."

"No, no, Kathy, we don't. But we *are* very concerned. It's been a week now."

Kathy rubbed her eyes and face in exhaustion. "I'll get over it. I just need some time, that's all."

"I think what you need is some sleep."

"Dan, I can't sleep."

"Oh, I know that. But that has me worried too. You should see yourself. You look like—"

"Please don't tell me how I look!"

Dan retreated. He even raised his hand a little as if to fend her off—then noticed, and dropped his hand immediately.

No. He couldn't lose her again; he couldn't let her retreat into her private pit, shutting him out. He felt like he was about to cry himself.

"Kathy . . ." he said quietly, desperately, "I really love you. I want you to know that."

She looked at him, maybe for the first time. "Do you really?"

Dan rose from his chair and sat on the sofa beside her, putting his arm around her and drawing her in. She welcomed his affection; she drank it in as she rested against him.

"I do love you," said Dan. "Really."

"Do you think I'm a good person?"

"You're the best."

Her lip began to quiver, and her head dropped.

"Hey, come on now," said Dan.

She quaked with her first sob. "I've always wanted to be good. I've always tried."

He touched her face. "You're a wonderful person. I wouldn't change a thing."

She just clung to him without a word. That was fine. He knew how to love her, and felt very comfortable doing that. They didn't need any more words, just time with each other. They took that time, and she seemed to rest a little easier.

He noticed the large book still in her lap. "What do you have here?"

She gave the album just a sideways glance. "Photo album."

He reached down and flipped it open. He had to smile. "Oh boy, here's some real history for you."

Kathy gave the album a little more attention.

They'd both seen these old photographs so many times before, but tonight it brought healing just to look at those cute little faces again, smiling, drooling, laughing. As always, it just didn't seem that long ago.

Little blonde Amy and her new wagon. Roughhouse Bruce with his sixth-grade soccer trophy. Tommy holding up his newly lost tooth.

A few pages back, they came across an old Christmas photo, and the kids were even smaller.

"How old were they when we took this?" asked Dan.

"That was in our old house in Hoodsport. Bruce had to be three, so Amy was only two."

"And Tommy . . . ?"

"I think I was still carrying him."

Dan turned the page.

Kathy chuckled at a very unflattering snapshot. "Boy, I sure was!"

Dan chuckled too. "You sure were." Then he shook his head. "Will you look at these little kids! Now Bruce is in college, Amy's a varsity cheerleader, Tommy's a . . ."

"A fifteen-year-old!"

"Yeah, right." They both laughed, and it was a welcome release. "Enough said."

They sat together on the sofa for a while, just enjoying each other's company, the quiet, and the peacefully passing time.

"Been thinking a lot about the kids lately?"

"Oh, I'm always thinking about the kids."

"Well, yeah, but . . ."

"But what?"

"Well, tonight it's the photo album, and last night you dug out all their old toys, and Tuesday night, didn't you sit up all night in the sewing room?"

"It was quiet in there."

Dan could feel the risk rising even as he said it. "Well, that used to be the nursery, remember?"

Kathy remained quiet. Now Dan felt awkward. Maybe he'd said too much.

"I was just . . . you know . . ." he fumbled.

"Was I a good mother?"

Dan spoke directly to her, sincerely. "Honey, you were great. You're still great. The kids have all turned out really well."

"Did I do all right?"

So the pain was still there. So now they'd have to keep talking about it.

"Sweetheart, really, when all is said and done, you don't have anything to regret. You don't have to go back and do anything over again."

Only a short moment later Kathy clapped the album shut. "I think I'll go to bed now."

The conversation was over. Dan felt relieved.

Kathy rose from the sofa and Dan stayed close by her. They went as a couple back to the bedroom.

"Thank you for loving me," she said.

"Don't ever worry about that," he answered.

Sometime in the early morning, Kathy finally lapsed into a fitful sleep. If Dan slept at all, he couldn't remember.

Three

I haven't used this razor in years, Dan thought, sloshing it around in the sink and hoping it was still sharp enough. Just keep it quiet, he thought, no matter what it takes. Let that woman sleep.

The can of shaving cream spat and sputtered into his palm. The shaving cream was limp and runny. The top of the can was getting rusty. Hoo boy, I hope I can even remember how to do this.

He was tired, he was cranky, and his thoughts weren't entirely clear this morning, but they were clear enough. He had plans for this day. He'd firmed them up in his mind just as daylight started coming through the window.

So I'll take the pain, he thought, or whatever it takes—I don't care anymore. Let's just get this thing resolved.

He heard footsteps outside the bathroom door. That would be Amy. She's up early.

She knocked very lightly.

He whispered, "Amy, keep it quiet. Mom's asleep."

The door cracked open and Amy looked in. Dan thought she bore very little resemblance to that baby picture they'd looked at last night . . . or actually this morning.

"She's *asleep?*" Amy whispered, her blue eyes widening. "You're kidding!"

"So tell Bruce and Tommy to keep it down. I don't want anything waking her up!"

A wry smile crossed her lips. "Is that why you're shaving with your old razor?"

He'd gotten in a few successful strokes already. "The electric one's too noisy."

Then Amy winced. "Oh brother. What about Tommy's radio?"

"He'll have to get along without it this morning, that's for sure. Why don't you sneak in there and unplug it?"

She liked that idea. "Okay."

"Oh, Amy . . ."

She stopped and poked her head in again.

"Listen, I've got to take off. Can you get Tommy moving and then run him by the school? I won't be going that way."

"You're not going to work today?"

"No, they'll just have to move some real estate

without me. I have some other things to take care of. Can you do that for me?"

"Sure."

"And I don't know what's going to happen with me or your mother today. She needs her sleep, and I don't know just when I'll be back . . ."

Amy lowered her voice even more and leaned in through the doorway. "Is this, uh . . . is everything all right?"

Dan didn't want to lie, but he thought about his answer. "We're working on a few things. It'll be okay."

Amy was just about to ask another question, but suddenly they both heard the sounds of a riot down the hall.

Tommy's radio.

Amy was gone in a flash, and Dan was off the hook.

Four

*K*athy thought the sound would go away, and she would continue to sleep, lying in the big bed, not moving, weighing tons, oblivious to the world. She was watching her dreams amble through her head, this way and that, from one picture to another, without sense or reason. It was perfect escape, perfect mindlessness. She could stay here forever.

But there was that sound again. Oh, it'll go away. I'll just keep dreaming.

Now the sound was ducking in and out of her dreams. It was an intrusion. It was unpleasant. It was . . . it was rude!

Come on, let's see the rest of this dream. Where did we leave off?

More of that sound. Children. That's what it was. Kids!

I don't have any little kids. None live around here. It's part of the dream.

It sounded like a playground. Hundreds of voices, all high-pitched, hollering, screaming, laughing.

I'm not awake, Kathy thought. I won't wake up. You can't do this to me.

She was aware of the pillow. She moved her hand and felt the sheets under her fingers. She was awake.

And there were kids playing outside her window!

Which means I can't be awake. This is still part of the dream. I don't have kids in my yard, not really.

She lay there a moment. She was awake. She was sure of it. Her bedroom was all around her, everything was in place. She could hear those kids outside. Now she was getting angry, which meant she had to be awake.

Those *kids* woke me up!

I can't believe this, I can't believe this—I didn't ask for it, I don't deserve it, somebody's in big trouble!

She rolled out of the bed and stood dizzily on her feet. The drapes were closed, and a dim, diffused daylight softly illuminated the room. What time was it?

Where was the clock? She leaned over the bed, trying to catch a glimpse of the little digital clock on the bedside table. It wasn't there. Dan must have moved it. Maybe Tommy borrowed it. They were going to hear about it.

She cracked the drapes open. The light stung her eyes, and she squinted them shut. It was blinding. She thought she saw *something* out there, something moving . . . But she had to give it up and let the drapes fall closed. Now there were purple blotches before her eyes. She groped for her robe and slippers and went to the door.

She felt a tinge of fear, a tightening in her stomach. Her eyes hurt again. The hallway had never looked liked this before, so brilliantly lit. Sunlight—if it was sunlight—poured into the house through every window, on every side. She stopped in the doorway, hesitant to take another step.

"Dan?"

No answer.

"Amy?"

The house was quiet and still—except for all those kids outside.

Her eyes grew accustomed to the light. Her fear left her quietly, without her even noticing. She started down the hall, glancing into the bathroom, the sewing room, Amy's room. Everyone was gone.

Her anger rose again. They'd all gone and left her alone with this problem, this invasion, this rude awakening! She marched into the kitchen, cornered tightly around the refrigerator . . . and then slowed to a stop just short of the sliding glass door. Brilliant daylight was streaming in, and she had to squint again, but she could see this time. She could see everything.

And she couldn't believe it.

Beyond that door, out beyond the deck, were all the playing children—*hundreds* of them! Kathy shaded her eyes with her hand. She couldn't make out the borders of her yard, nor could she see the back fence. All she could see was that living, scrambling, frolicking sea of little kids.

She put her hand on the door handle, built up the nerve, and slid the door open.

The children didn't seem to notice or mind her appearance. They just kept playing, running, throwing balls, skipping about, tagging each other, climbing in the fruit trees, and causing a terrible commotion.

Kathy went to the deck railing. Under all those little running bodies there was a lawn begging for mercy. This all had to be stopped.

"Hey!"

Some kids noticed her at last. The rest had races to win, balls to catch, opponents to tag, trees to climb.

"Hey!"

A hush began to work its way from the front to the back of the crowd as the tumult receded like a tide. Hundreds of little eyes were looking up at her and paying remarkably good attention. Kathy would have been impressed with their courtesy, but she was too angry.

"What are all you kids doing in my yard?" she

asked, her voice raised out of anger, and also to reach the back rows. "You know, you're right outside my bedroom there and I was trying to sleep! Now I want all of you . . . well . . ."

The words dropped from her mind and she couldn't retrieve them. What was she doing? She . . . well, she was addressing a throng of hundreds of children, all in her backyard for no apparent reason.

The children were still listening, waiting for her to speak again. She had to look them all over, from the motley soccer players on the left side to the hop-scotchers over on the right, from the little fat faces in front to the tree conquerors clear in the back. They were real enough. They looked like any bunch of kids on any school playground. They were white, black, oriental, small, big, cute, ugly, shy, exuberant, the whole gamut.

There was only one thing truly wrong: she had their full attention.

Kathy found some words and quickly stumbled into them before she lost this precious moment. "I . . . I want to know where all you kids came from, just tell me that."

One little fellow in the front answered her quickly and clearly. "We live here."

No, no, that wasn't a satisfactory answer at all. "What do you mean, you *live* here?"

A little black girl simply repeated the answer, totally satisfied with it. "We live here."

A tall, thin boy backed them up. "Yeah, all of us do."

Kathy shook her head and held up her hand to stop any more such answers. "No, no, now listen to me. This is *my* house, and this is *my* yard, and you do not live *here!*"

A little blondie chirped, "We live *around* here."

The others that heard her chuckled and giggled. They thought that should clear it up.

It didn't as far as Kathy was concerned. "Well, I doubt that! I've never seen any of you in this neighborhood before, much less *all* of you. Did you come here from the school or something?"

Now they just looked at each other dumbly. Kathy selected the tall, thin boy to confront on this one. "Young man, I asked you a question!"

He gave her a double take and asked, "Me?"

"Yes, you! What's your name?"

"My . . . my name?" he asked.

Kathy couldn't believe it. She'd stumped him.

"You heard me!"

He started to think about it really hard. He even looked at his friends for help. One little fellow whispered some suggestions to him.

"Well," he finally answered, "I guess I don't have a name."

Kids all around him giggled.

Kathy didn't think it was funny. She thought it was rude and impudent. "Well, maybe I'll just have to talk to your parents, huh? Do you want me to do that?"

That didn't seem to threaten him; instead, it stumped him again. He looked at his friends and they muttered something back, shaking their heads and shrugging.

He looked up at her, sorry to have to tell her, "I don't have any parents either, ma'am."

Kathy was about to jump over the rail. "Are you trying to be a smart aleck—"

"It's true, ma'am!" the little blonde girl pleaded. "We don't have any parents!"

"None of us do," said her little black friend.

All right, blondie, since you seem to know so much— "And just who are you?"

"I'm . . . well, I'm me."

Her friend tried to help her. "Sometimes we call her Blue Eyes."

Kathy pointed her finger right at the little nose. "I want to know your *name!*"

The little girl answered pleadingly, "I don't have a name either!"

Kathy leaned back from the rail. She was beginning to believe all this, and that unnerved her. "No names . . . and no parents? All of you?"

They all nodded, chirped yeses, and agreed. They were very relieved that she was finally catching on.

"But that doesn't make a bit of sense, and you know it . . . and I *still* don't know where you came from!"

"Well," one brave little fellow ventured, "we were sort of wondering where *you* came from."

They all piped up their agreement with that question.

I'm not getting anywhere, Kathy thought. Much more of this and I'll go crazy.

"All right," she shouted over their babbling, "that's it! That's enough! That does it! Now I want all of you—and I don't care who you are—to get out of my yard, right this minute! Go on, now!"

The tide of little bodies began to go out; the lawn in front of the deck began to reappear. The children didn't seem too indignant or sassy about it. They obeyed right away, flowing outward from the yard in all directions.

Kathy still had some steam to vent. "Hey! You two over there! You skedaddle! And you kids get out of that tree, you're going to break a limb! Go on now!"

The kids dropped from the trees like ripe fruit and scattered with all the others.

Kathy grasped the deck rail. At least it was something solid, something she could use to orient herself with the real world—if it was the real world. What she had just seen and heard could not have been real, but everything else seemed real enough. The deck was there, just like always, as were the house and the yard. She didn't feel dizzy or drunk or drugged; she was quite sure she had her wits about her.

There's an explanation, she told herself. It's just some strange fluke. I'll bet Dan's got some big brainstorm going, some super promotional scheme, and he just forgot to tell me about it. I've been so out of touch anyway, he could have told me and I didn't hear him. Sure. When he gets home, I'll find out about it.

She put her hand on the door handle. I've got to just get my day started. It'll all make sense soon enough.

Then her eye caught a small glimpse of white, and she looked purely out of reflex. Oh brother, a straggler.

It was a little girl in white, a pale scarf arranged in her long, jet-black hair. She was sitting, almost hiding on the bottom step of the back stairs. When their eyes met, she looked down sheepishly, but then, with an apologetic air, looked at Kathy again. She'd been crying, and her eyes were still wet.

For a moment neither said a word, and neither looked away.

Kathy had a little trouble building up a firm voice. "Well, what are you still doing here?"

The little girl must have been right on the edge—immediately her big eyes winced, her lip quivered, and she dropped her head, bursting into tears.

Kathy hurried to the steps, her fuzzy slippers scuffing over the boards. "Sweetheart, are you all right?"

The child was trying desperately to compose herself. She could barely get the words out clearly. "Yes, thank you."

Kathy made her way down the steps. "Did you fall on the steps or something?"

Almost like a frightened bird, the little girl got quickly to her feet and backed away just a little. She wiped her eyes with her fingers, then wiped her fingers on her dress. "I'm all right." She drew a deep breath. "I just wanted to look."

Kathy slowed her movements, sat quietly on the steps, and made a conscious effort to soften her tone and expression. She had no desire to frighten the child. She smiled pleasantly. "Uh . . . look at what?"

The child blinked away some more tears and tried to hold down some more sobbing. "At you . . ."

"Oh, now don't cry. It's all right . . ." Kathy reached out and just barely touched the little shoulder, just lightly felt the soft, white muslin.

"I'm fine, really," said the little girl.

46

Kathy didn't hear the words with her full attention. "You're not hurt?" she asked half-mindedly.

The little girl shook her head. Some of her long locks brushed against Kathy's hand. Kathy withdrew her hand.

No words would come. Kathy kept looking at the child and hoped she wasn't staring, but the child seemed to be staring just as much at her.

Well, Kathy, say something! "Uh . . . is there anything I can do for you?"

The big brown eyes were full of longing, and explored Kathy's face as the little girl composed an answer.

"Do you think . . ." She hesitated, looked away to build some more strength, then continued, "I could please . . ."

Kathy smiled just to comfort her. "Well, what?"

The brown eyes filled with resolve. "I would really like to have lunch with you, in your house."

Kathy chuckled. "Oh, sweetheart . . ." Strangely, the idea was very inviting. But no. This really couldn't be. "Listen, that isn't my job. I'm . . . well, I'm a stranger. You need to go home and have lunch in your own house, with your own family." Family. Kathy remembered what all the other children had said. "You do *live* around here, don't you?"

"Uh-huh."

47

Kathy rose deliberately to her feet. This meeting had to end. "So, all right, that's where you need to go. You let your folks take care of that . . ." She didn't want to ask, but then she did. "Unless you don't have any . . ."

The child always looked her right in the eye. "I might."

"You might?" Kathy felt like she was being teased, baited. "Well, tell you what, why don't you go home and find out for sure? How about it?"

She extended her hand to help the little girl along, but hoped the gesture would be enough. She didn't want to touch her.

The child started to back away, not out of fear, but out of obedience.

"It was nice to meet you, ma'am," she said.

"It was nice to meet you too, uh . . ." Oh, that's right, these kids don't have names. Kathy sighed to herself and turned toward the stairs.

"Tilly," said the girl.

Kathy's foot rested on the first step and remained there. Her hand grasped the railing. She didn't want to turn around. What if that little girl was still standing there? What if she wasn't?

Kathy looked over her shoulder.

The little girl named Tilly was still there, her brown eyes returning Kathy's gaze. The bright daylight played on the muslin; the dress seemed to glow.

Kathy turned around, hoping it would not frighten the child. The little girl seemed ready enough to leave if so ordered, but for now she was waiting, watching Kathy.

Kathy approached the girl as if approaching a timid animal and stooped beside her. She touched the little shoulder again.

"Sweetheart . . ." It was so difficult to speak. "Could you tell me . . . who gave you that name?"

"I don't know. I've just always been called that."

"And why did you want to look at me?"

Tilly looked down—but only for a moment—in embarrassment. "I'm sorry. I just wanted to look at your face."

And she was still looking. Kathy didn't notice that much; she was looking at Tilly.

"Tilly . . . would you happen to know . . . how old you are?"

"Nine, I think."

"Nine."

Kathy found herself stroking the black hair, soft and clean under her fingers. "And you really want to have lunch with me?"

Tilly's face brightened at the possibility. "Yes, please, if I could."

Kathy sighed in resignation. "Well . . . then I'd

really like to have the pleasure of your company at lunch today. Would you like to come?"

Tilly nodded, and it was almost a curtsy. "I'd be very happy to, thank you."

Kathy rose and extended her hand toward the stairs. "Then won't you come in?"

They went into the house together.

Five

$\mathcal{T}$he old mowing machine roared up and down, around and around, dodging between the gravestones, down one row, up the next as the old caretaker followed the same intricate course he'd followed for years. Perhaps imagining he was in a race or running an obstacle course, he felt like a teenager riding a hot racing machine. It was all part of enjoying his work, doing it well, his way.

He liked listening to the roar of the engine, the rattle of the fenders, the whirring of the blades. They all told him how well the machine was doing, and he was sensitive to that; he'd kept this old machine running like a fine watch for years.

But now . . . what was that other sound? Was something coming loose? Must be the idler pulley on the third blade. Drat! I just replaced that thing!

There it was again.

He slowed the engine and eased the mower to a

stop so he could listen to it idling and rattling, the muffler pounding out little puffs of exhaust like a steady drum roll. Now what's wrong here?

"Hello!" came the sound. "Hey there!"

Oh, it's somebody hollering!

He looked around and saw a man running up from behind, gasping for air like a drowning man. Heh! I wonder how long he was back there hollering at me.

"Well," said the caretaker, "hi there! Nice morning, eh?"

Dan Ross finally caught up, still trying to catch his breath, and extended his hand. "Hi. Sorry to bother you like this . . ."

"Hey, don't worry about it. I'm glad all that noise was you and not the mower here. Oh, hang on." He reached down and turned off the ignition. Suddenly the world was deathly, strangely quiet. "There. Now what can I do for you?"

"My name is Dan Ross, and I was at a funeral here a week ago."

The old man's eyes brightened. "Oh, sure! You buried old Frank Smith, right?"

Dan was impressed. "Well, yes, that's right. You have quite a memory."

"Oh, I just pay attention, that's all. If you're gonna work here, you gotta know who's buried where and who the newcomers are."

"Well, sure, right. Then you ought to be able to help me. I'm trying to find a particular grave. We walked by it last week, but I can't remember exactly where it was."

"What was the name?"

"Uh . . . Tilly. That's all it said."

The caretaker didn't have the slightest trouble remembering that one. He nodded his head knowingly and hopped off the mower. "Right this way, right over here. You picked one I know quite well. It's the kind you don't forget."

Dan followed the little man as he hurried across rows of graves, giving Dan a little bit of a tour.

"Yep," he said, "some of these graves date back to the 1800s. They're pretty lonely now; no one left to come and see them. Now these here are newer . . . Some of them I knew myself. Here's Portia Weberly, and here's Amos, her husband. They used to run that cider shop up on Wingate. Ever been in there?"

"Well, no, I—"

"Timothy Stewart, a young boy who got killed in Vietnam. I know his folks, Gus and Molly. Nice people. These plots are for them, right next to their boy. Don't suppose you remember the Blundquists, Henry and Irma?"

"The Blundquists?"

"Oo, they need weeding, will you look at that?"

Dan tried to be polite. He hesitated to properly assess the weed situation.

The caretaker was way ahead of him. "Yeah, right here. Is this the one you're after?"

Dan turned from the Blundquists and hurried to where the caretaker was standing.

There it was, a small stone, so insignificant and so easily lost among all the others—except for the caretaker who remembered.

"This is it," said Dan. He felt just a little hesitant to ask, "What can you tell me about it?"

The caretaker's mood changed. He didn't hurry through this one. "This was one of the really sad ones. Tilly was just a baby, a tiny baby. I mean, that casket was no bigger than a shoe box. Yeah, it was really sad."

"Well . . . what about the parents? I mean, last week we saw a woman here."

"Ah, Mrs. Mendoza."

"You know her?"

"I know her name, don't remember how. But she comes here every April to put flowers on the grave, steady as the seasons."

"That had to be her then."

"She's a strange sort. Pretty quiet."

Dan could remember the poor woman running away in what looked like stark terror. "She did seem rather timid."

"That she is. She's never said boo to me. I don't know much about her at all."

"Would you have any idea of how I might contact her?"

The caretaker had to consider that for a moment. "Can't say that I do . . . She might be in the phone book . . ."

"I suppose so."

"But let me tell you . . . I think you might be wiser to talk to the funeral home first. I seem to recall the Bendix brothers being involved in the thing."

"Bendix . . ."

"2203 Medford, right across from the Baptist church, the one with the big iron bell tower."

"Oh, right, mm-hmm."

"Yeah, they were here that day, I'm almost positive. You'd be wise to talk to them."

Dan didn't ask why. He simply said, "Well, thank you very much," and extended his hand again.

The caretaker took Dan's hand and gave it a firm shake, never taking his eyes off him. "No problem, Dan Ross. Glad to help."

Dan turned and started walking away.

The caretaker called after him, "Oh, listen, if you're gonna start talking this around, would you leave me out of it?"

"Don't worry," Dan answered. "I'll keep it quiet. And thanks again."

"You're welcome," the old man replied. Then he looked down at the little gravestone and said quietly to himself, "I'm glad I met you, Dan Ross." He rehearsed the name again. "Dan Ross . . ."

Six

$\mathcal{A}$re you through?" Kathy asked her prim little guest.

Tilly daintily wiped her mouth with her napkin and replied, "Yes, thank you. It was delicious!"

"Finish your milk."

Tilly complied quickly.

Kathy was amazed at what a pleasant lunch they'd had. There simply had been no baby-sitting involved. Tilly was a perfect guest. "Well, for a little girl who may or may not have any parents, you have very good manners, Miss Tilly."

"Thank you. And the soup and sandwich were excellent!"

Kathy's heart was more than adequately warmed. "Thank you very much."

They sat together in the dinette just off the kitchen. It was a special time; Kathy had spread the table with her favorite linen and her best china and silver. It just seemed the thing to do.

"You must be a wonderful mother, Mrs. Ross."

"Well . . ."

"Do Bruce and Amy and Tommy think you're a good mother?"

"Oh, yes."

"Do you have lunch with them too?"

"Oh . . . well, not too often. They're away at school most of the time, and then they're always running around a lot . . ."

Tilly seemed so disappointed. "I'd always want to eat lunch with you, and dinner too."

Kathy laughed. "Well, we don't always have meals quite this fancy."

"But you'd be there!"

Kathy was touched. She looked into those big brown eyes that just seemed to be drinking her in, and couldn't think of anything to say. It was wondrous—and unsettling. She looked away, checked for the time . . .

The clock on the wall . . . wasn't on the wall.

"What in the world . . . ?"

Tilly was quite alarmed. "What is it, Mrs. Ross? What's the matter?"

Kathy looked around the room. "I can't find the clock."

"What's a clock?"

"What's a . . . ? Oh . . . well, it's a . . . It's how we tell what time it is."

"What's that?"

Just when things were getting comfortable, now this. She tried to brush it aside. "Oh, it doesn't matter." She rose from the table. "Can I get you anything else?"

"Oh, no more for me, thanks." Then Tilly got alarmed again. "Mrs. Ross? Are you all right?"

Kathy was staring out the window. "Um . . . yes, Tilly. I'm fine. I was just looking outside . . ."

"It's pretty, isn't it?"

Kathy went to the window and Tilly joined her.

Outside the window, the world had changed.

"There used to be a big chestnut tree out there," Kathy said quietly, "and a picnic bench, and our old doghouse, and our fence . . . and the Cramers' house just next door . . ."

Now there were only green meadows on rolling hills, towering trees with dancing leaves, and flowers, millions of flowers.

"This isn't my neighborhood," Kathy realized.

"No," said Tilly rather simply, "this is my neighborhood."

Kathy touched the edge of the window. It was still solid. "This is my house."

"Yes. I like it."

"But what is my house doing in your neighborhood?"

Tilly was troubled. "Don't you want to be here?"

Kathy closed her eyes for a moment. At least inside her eyelids she was in control. *None of this is right; I'm dreaming or something.*

"Mrs. Ross?" came Tilly's voice.

A dream. It's okay, Kathy, it's all just a dream. You know how wild dreams can get.

"Mrs. Ross?"

"Hm?" she said.

"What's your husband's name?"

"Dan."

"Is he a nice man?"

Kathy opened her eyes and looked at Tilly. She was still there. She was real. She was waiting for an answer.

"Um . . . well, yes. Yes, he's a very nice man." She decided to answer better. "He's a *wonderful* man."

"Does he love you a whole lot?"

Kathy was proud to answer, "Yes, a whole lot, and I love him too."

Tilly received that like a gift, lighting up the room with her smile. "What does he look like?"

They were talking about real things, and it felt right. "Oh, well, let me show you some pictures. See in there?"

Kathy pointed into the living room, and Tilly hurried in that direction. Tilly's eyes were filled with wonder, even reverence, as she saw the many photographs on the wall, the table, and the mantel.

Kathy touched a large photograph on one side of the mantel. "This is my man, right here."

Tilly studied the face, her eyes taking it in little by little, one careful portion at a time. At first her mouth hung open in awe, and then, with joy and satisfaction she broke into a smile, nodding in happy approval.

"I like the way he looks. He likes to smile, doesn't he?"

"Oh, yes," said Kathy, looking for a careful second time at Tilly's smile. "That was one of the first things I noticed about him."

Tilly moved to another picture, this one hanging on the wall. "Oh . . . is that *you?*"

"Yes. This is our wedding picture."

"Your wedding!" Tilly studied that picture for a moment, and then looked back and forth from Kathy to the picture. "You're just so pretty!"

Kathy felt embarrassed and flattered. "Oh . . ."

"I've never been to a wedding, but I get to go to one pretty soon."

"Oh, really?" Kathy was glad to hear at least a

trace of normal conversation about something normal happening around here. "Who's getting married?"

"*Jesus* is getting married."

That caught Kathy off-guard, but she was delighted. "Oh, do you know about Jesus?"

"Oh yes. He lives up the road. I think He's a very important person because lots of people come to see Him all the time. But He still plays with me and tells me stories."

So much for normal.

Tilly went on to the next picture. "Oh . . . let me guess. Is this Bruce?"

Kathy felt pulled along, as if she was straggling. "Oh, um, sure, that's him. That's his graduation picture."

"Is he nice like you, and like Mr. Dan Ross?"

"He really is. He's grown up to be a fine young man. And that's—"

"Amy, right?"

"Right. She's a senior in high school. And that's . . ." Kathy waited for Tilly to guess.

"Tommy."

"Right. He's in the ninth grade."

Tilly was almost dancing with excitement, darting from one picture to another, studying the faces, looking from them to Kathy and back again.

"So . . ." Kathy ventured, "uh . . . Jesus . . . What was that you said . . . ?"

But Kathy put aside the question. Tilly had become motionless in the center of the room, transfixed, gazing up at a large family portrait over the mantel. There, dressed in their best, huddled closely, and all smiling was the Ross family: Dan, Kathy, Bruce, Amy, and Tommy. The child covered her mouth with her fingers.

Kathy spoke softly, as if the moment had somehow become sacred. "That's all of us together. We had that taken just last month."

"All of you . . . together," Tilly repeated.

Kathy stood beside Tilly and looked at the picture. Perhaps she had never looked at it so long and so carefully before. Her children all had such bright, brown eyes; their smiles were so warm and cheerful. Kathy looked down at Tilly again. She hoped the child wouldn't notice her staring.

"Would you like to get closer?"

Tilly hardly broke her gaze. "Do you think I could?"

Kathy brought a wooden chair and set it against the mantel. She took Tilly's hand and helped her up. "All right?"

"Yes. Thank you."

Tilly lightly touched the frame of the picture as she looked at each face. She hated to blink, but she had to. She looked away just long enough to dab tears from her eyes with her sleeve.

Kathy could see the child's face so close now to the faces of her family. Suddenly the image blurred.

"Don't cry, Mrs. Ross," came Tilly's broken voice.

Kathy blinked the tears away and grabbed an excuse. "Well, I saw *you* crying."

Tilly tried to smile even while the tears ran down her face. "I can't help it. You all just look so wonderful."

Kathy hurried to bring a Kleenex. She gave it to Tilly and then lovingly placed her hand on the little girl's shoulder.

"Tilly," she asked very gently, "where is *your* family?"

Tilly finished wiping her nose and answered, "Jesus takes care of me."

Kathy tried to smile. Her vision was blurring again. "Honey, of course Jesus takes care of all of us, but—"

"—and all my friends, too."

"The other children?"

"Uh-huh."

"But . . . Tilly, who are they? Where did they come from?"

Tilly wouldn't look at Kathy now. "I don't know. I guess they're all just like me. They came here, and they didn't have any parents, and most of them didn't have any names, and they didn't know anything about where they came from."

"Tilly . . ." Kathy drew very close. Would Tilly's eyes meet hers? Tilly looked at her. "You really don't know where you came from?"

Tilly's eyes went immediately to the picture. She smiled again. "Mrs. Ross, tell me about Amy. Is she fun to talk to? Does she like to play outside?"

Kathy answered the question only because Tilly had asked it. "Amy's been a runner and player since she was smaller than you. She's a bundle of energy."

"What does she like to do?"

So now we're on to another subject. Okay. "Well . . . oh, what *doesn't* she do? She cheerleads, she swims, she hikes, she sings, and she paints too. She's really quite an artist."

"Can I see her room, Mrs. Ross?"

"Sure."

Kathy helped Tilly down from the chair. Tilly was ready to do some more exploring.

"Can I see your whole house, Mrs. Ross? Can I see Amy's room, and Tommy's room, and your room?"

"Come on, I'll give you the grand tour."

"And what about Tommy? Tell me about him. What does he like to do?"

They headed toward the hallway and toward the

back of the house where the rooms took on the personalities of their owners and every detail had a precious story behind it.

"You'd like Tommy," Kathy said, trying to keep up with Tilly's voracious curiosity. "He's a real character. He's real funny, always running all over the place with all kinds of schemes and projects going . . . I guess he'll be quite an athlete, like his brother. Of course, I'd say that Bruce is more of a deep thinker . . ."

Tilly listened to it all, and kept asking for more.

Seven

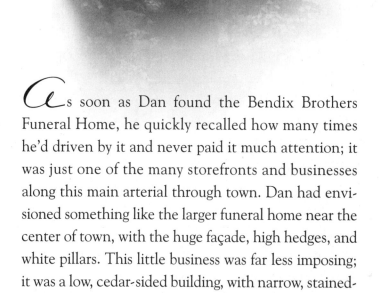

$\mathcal{A}$s soon as Dan found the Bendix Brothers Funeral Home, he quickly recalled how many times he'd driven by it and never paid it much attention; it was just one of the many storefronts and businesses along this main arterial through town. Dan had envisioned something like the larger funeral home near the center of town, with the huge façade, high hedges, and white pillars. This little business was far less imposing; it was a low, cedar-sided building, with narrow, stained-glass windows and a simple, black-topped driveway lined with carefully pruned rose bushes. It looked more like a small community church than a funeral home. Dan actually felt a little relieved.

He stood at the front door for a moment. Do I knock or do I just go in? Finally he did both; he knocked lightly, then opened the door just a crack, knocked lightly again, then stuck his head in. Oh. This was just like the foyer of a church, and no one was around. He stepped inside and closed the door very quietly behind him. Through a wide double door he could see the small chapel, warm, serene, and inviting, but deserted.

At the left end of the foyer was an unmarked door, but it looked like an important door, so Dan went to it and knocked again.

A distinguished-looking older man opened the door.

"Oh, hello there," the man said. "Are you Mr. Ross?"

He had to be the undertaker; his gentle and consoling manner must have come with that dark, pin-striped suit and those little wire-framed glasses.

"Yes. And are you the Mr. Bendix I spoke to on the phone?"

The little man flashed several gold fillings. "Ah yes, yes! Won't you come in?"

Mr. Bendix swung the door widely open, almost with a flourish, and Dan passed through it feeling like an honored guest. He wondered if he would be so regarded when he left this place.

Bendix showed him into his neat little office, actually a little cubicle by the window. "Please have a seat. Would you like some coffee?"

Dan didn't really want any. "Oh yes, thank you."

"Cream and sugar?"

"Uh . . . black. Just black, please."

Mr. Bendix poured the coffee from a little coffeemaker in the corner. "Now . . . you said something on the phone about a particular funeral we may have had . . . oh, what was it? Nine years ago?"

"Yes . . ." Dan took a cup from Mr. Bendix. "Thank you. I don't know if you keep records that far back, but . . ." Dan knew he'd just have to take that big step. "I was wondering if you might recall a service for a very small infant."

Mr. Bendix settled into his chair and reflected back over the years. He nodded his head sadly. "We have had a few of those. Those are particularly tragic, very difficult."

Dan could feel the very thin ice under him, but he pressed on. "Well . . . I was thinking of a funeral that may have involved someone by the name of Mendoza. A woman named Mendoza."

Bendix remembered. Dan could see it.

Mr. Bendix looked at Dan, then down at his desk, and then at Dan again. "Could I . . . venture to ask just what your motivation might be in seeking this information?"

Dan just pressed him further. "Do you remember it?"

"Oh yes, I remember it. But you need to understand, Mr. Ross, that there are some ethical considerations here. It wouldn't be proper to violate Mrs. Mendoza's privacy."

"What *can* you tell me?"

Dan was trying to be gentle and polite, but he just couldn't be turned away. He kept his eyes on Bendix.

The gentleman was apologetic. "If I were to tell you anything, I could be making a serious mistake."

"You won't be."

Mr. Bendix rubbed his chin and looked over his glasses at Dan.

"All right," he said. "I will tell you only what I think I can. I can tell you that it took place in April nine years ago." Then his eyes drifted toward the ceiling as he began to recall it. "Yes, it was April. It's still very vivid in my mind because it was so different . . . It was different, and so very difficult."

Dan watched Mr. Bendix intensely. The gentleman seemed to be living the event all over again.

Mr. Bendix recalled, "I remember . . . Mrs. Mendoza's pastor approaching us, and I remember we made the arrangements with him. We were given the remains the same day." He stopped short. He gazed at Dan, trying to read his eyes. "Would it surprise you, Mr. Ross, to know what an unusual case it was? There was no certificate of death; there was no certificate of birth. We handled the whole case very quietly, as I'm sure you understand. You see . . ." With this,

Bendix stopped again. He leaned his face on his straight, nervous fingers and let his eyes drop. "Mr. Ross, the child's death had been intentional. It was very small, not even full-term, and the body was burned and scarred. I was quite frankly at a loss when confronted with such a thing, but something inside me responded; I felt that there was a right thing to do, and that I had to carry it out.

"I ordered a special casket from our supplier, but even then it was oversized . . ." Mr. Bendix removed his glasses and rubbed his eyes, lost in the memory. "And I'll never forget it. The minister conducted a simple service with just a brief message, a few words from Scripture . . . And I can still remember him standing there over that little casket, with no other person in the chapel but . . . Mrs. Mendoza. She was sitting in the second row, dressed in black, all by herself, weeping."

Mr. Bendix found a tissue and began cleaning his glasses, whether they needed it or not. "Mr. Ross, this is my business, my profession, to give comfort and serve families in their time of sorrow and need. I do care, but still I don't get emotionally affected by what I see in that chapel. But this . . . this was something quite different, and I've never seen the like of it before or since then. A woman . . . terminating her pregnancy . . . and then mourning for that child, and giving that child a funeral. It was *very* unsettling, very shattering. I'll never forget it."

Mr. Bendix paused just a moment. He seemed to be snapping out of the spell, coming back from his disturbing recollections. He quickly replaced his glasses.

"Mr. Ross," he said, "I hope I've answered some of your questions."

Dan had heard enough. He wasn't sure how to respond to Mr. Bendix. He had no words, no replies. He only wanted to get out of there.

"Mr. Bendix . . . I'm very satisfied with what you've told me. You've done me a great service." Bendix gave a slight nod. "I guess the next thing I need to know is the name of that minister, Mrs. Mendoza's pastor. Could you share that with me?"

Mr. Bendix knew it without looking it up. "Reverend Michael O'Cleary. He's at the Neighborhood Chapel, just up the street, two blocks, on the right. He should be there now."

Eight

Mrs. Ross? Would you hold my hand? I want you to hold my hand and walk with me."

Kathy took the soft little hand in hers as they stood in the fresh, scented air. With a conscious resolve, she turned her back on the house and looked toward the entirely new and perfect landscape that surrounded them on every side. She took her first step toward that world, eager to see it, learn of it, somehow partake of the peace that filled it. She kept walking, aware of each step, still hand in hand with the child, somehow knowing that the house, that fine suburban house, her only link with the natural, the day-to-day, the routine, would not be there should she look back. She was passing from one world to another, giving herself over to a dream that was too real to be a dream.

The meadow grass waved gently in a slow ballet, and the flowers nodded their greeting. The path was soft loam beneath their feet, warm and comfortable. Kathy accepted it and just watched, observed, learned.

The trees that towered above them were strong, their limbs ponderous and expressive, their high crowns protective and sheltering. Birds were everywhere, from tiny to large, all splashed with brilliant color, filling the air with melodic song and landing on branches surprisingly close to warble their joy to their visitors.

Then Tilly, as if joining the chorus of the birds, began to sing in a very sweet tone, her spirit speaking in a gentle and playful tune, with notes tumbling and frolicking like children on a hillside. She sang boldly, clearly, and her eyes danced, shining with the special light that filled this place, that seemed to come from everywhere.

Kathy listened and watched; she said no word and made no move that might break this precious and delicate picture. This was blessing embodied in a little child; this was joy, life, and purity. There was no sorrow here. Pain was far away.

Tilly ended her song and looked up at Kathy. Kathy could feel her little hand squeezing hers, and there was that smile again.

"That was beautiful, Miss Tilly! Thank you very much."

Tilly just giggled.

"Do you like to sing a lot?"

"Oh, everybody sings around here."

"So I noticed." Then Kathy ventured, "You must be very happy here."

But Tilly suddenly had a thought that took precedence over any others. "You know what? We found the biggest tree that there ever was, and nobody's even climbed to the top of it yet! That's what I'm going to do! I'm going to climb clear to the top!"

"Oh, I'm sure you will. What else do you like to do?"

"Um . . . I like to make up stories just like Jesus does. My friends and I can't wait to tell each other stories. But Jesus tells stories better than anybody."

Kathy accepted that. She believed it. It was all part of the dream—or the reality. She dared not question which it might be.

The path descended lazily into a small valley, and they could hear the laughing sound of a creek. Kathy could see the sparkles and splashes through the trees, and then she could make out the creek itself, meandering and winding through the woods, the light bounding off its little waves in thousands of dazzling rainbows.

They came to a bridge, a special bridge. It was small, arched, and . . . not made of planks, boards, or rails. It was living; it had grown there. Each end was rooted in the rich soil, and the siderails were festooned with bright green, hand-sized leaves. Kathy had to pause and have a good look at this.

"This is my favorite bridge," Tilly announced.

"I can see why."

"Come on across."

Kathy let Tilly pull her along over the little bridge. Kathy was watching the dancing light from the creek, fascinated by the sight.

And then she saw the stones lining the creek bed. Now she knew she had to stop. Tilly was tugging her hand.

"Wait, wait."

Tilly joined her at the rail. "Huh?"

Kathy knew Tilly would not be surprised, but she couldn't help her own feelings. "Tilly . . . those are jewels down there . . ."

Tilly smiled. "Yes. They're pretty, aren't they?"

"Look at that gold . . . and those rubies and emeralds . . ."

"Come over here," Tilly said, walking ahead. "I'll show you my favorite spot."

Kathy followed the little girl from the bridge and onto a grassy knoll overlooking the shimmering creek of jewels. It was an ideal spot. The ground was warm and welcoming, the grass like a thick carpet. All around them, the rainbow light from the creek played on the trees, and the sound of the rippling water filled the air.

They sat down, and they were quiet. Kathy wanted to see everything. She wanted to know this place. Tilly gave her all the time she needed.

"Tilly . . . it's a wonderful place."

Tilly only smiled.

The sight of this little girl in this wondrous setting brought back a question. "Tilly, you must be very happy here."

Tilly looked down and played with some blades of grass. "Mostly . . ."

"Just . . . mostly?"

Tilly looked far away, across the creek, maybe toward the house that was no longer there. She sighed a little sigh, and looked down again as she said softly, "I want to see my family, Mrs. Ross."

Kathy was silent for a moment. Tilly had just shared something so priceless, so special. O Lord, don't let me bruise that little heart.

She dared to ask one more question. "Then . . . you *do* have a family?"

Tilly wouldn't look up, but played with the blades of grass, thinking, feeling. Then, finally, she nodded. "Jesus told me about them. But they're not here."

"Did He tell you about your parents?"

"Yes."

Kathy felt she was invading, going too far. Part of

her wanted to retreat, to let this little girl just keep her secrets.

But the question came out, even as Kathy regretted it. "What did He say?"

Tilly tried to look at Kathy, but couldn't, and her eyes found the blades of grass again. "He . . . told me their names, and He told me what they're like . . . and He said I'll get to see them someday and we'll all be together." Her voice started to waver, but she resolutely pushed out the words. "But sometimes . . . I just can't wait, I want to see them so bad!"

One more question, little child? Just one more? "Tilly . . ."

But Tilly looked up. "Mrs. Ross, I'm sure glad you came to visit. I wish you could stay here all the time."

And Kathy eased back. "Sweetheart . . . I don't even know how I got here, but I'm very thankful that I did. I'm very pleased to have met you."

Tilly fumbled with the blades of grass, looked away, then finally met Kathy's eyes and asked, "Do you think you could love me, Mrs. Ross?"

Kathy would have embraced the little girl right then and there, but she didn't. She couldn't. But she did say, "Tilly . . . I know I could love you."

Nine

$\mathcal{P}$astor Michael O'Cleary spoke some instructions to his secretary. "Janet, please hold any calls. Mr. Ross and I are not to be disturbed."

Then he quietly closed the door to his office, shutting out the world, closing himself in with a very quiet, very troubled man.

"Won't you sit down, Mr. Ross?"

Dan mumbled a very weak thank you and found a chair without another word.

O'Cleary pulled up another chair and sat close to him. "I'm glad you dropped by, uh . . . can I call you Dan?"

"Sure."

O'Cleary leaned forward and spoke in a quiet, clear voice. "Dan . . . ever since a particular day nine years ago, I often wondered if this meeting of ours would take place. Obviously there had to be other parties involved."

"I guess you know why I'm here."

"Well . . . it seems we have a mutual friend. Anita Mendoza?"

Dan gave a weak smile and nodded.

O'Cleary returned a smile just to set him at ease. "Mrs. Mendoza belongs to my congregation, and she did share your name with me. It was just this week, as a matter of fact. She was very distraught over a chance meeting she'd had with you and your wife at the cemetery."

Dan let his head sink into one hand. "Go on. I'll listen."

"Do you remember Anita?"

"Hardly at all. It was just a hunch, I guess. I just thought it had to be . . ."

"Well, she remembers you and Kathy extremely well. She just didn't know what to say when she encountered you there at the grave. She felt terrible for running, but . . . she felt there was nothing else she could do."

Dan looked at the minister and regained his resolve. He was sure he knew the answer even as he asked the question. "Is she a nurse?"

O'Cleary played right along. "She's a registered nurse, yes."

"Did she ever work at the Family Planning Clinic down on Bedford and Eighth?"

O'Cleary paused just enough for effect. "Nine years ago."

Dan stopped. He was too stunned to continue.

Then, with a decision, he let go of his feelings and the tears started, hot against his face, released at last, at long last.

O'Cleary put his hand on Dan's shoulder. He said nothing, but Dan could feel the man's comforting touch and he was glad for it.

"We never talked about it," Dan said. "I knew she was hurting from it. I was too, but it's just . . . it's just too big, too scary, you don't want to go near it. You just try to bury it and hope it'll go away. For nine years we've never talked about it. We used to talk about everything; we always knew what we were thinking. But now we don't. It's like a rule with us."

"Until the cemetery . . ."

"It did something to Kathy. She couldn't sleep at night, she wouldn't talk to me or the kids, she . . . she just wasn't herself. I knew it had to be that gravestone. I didn't know why . . . or maybe I just wouldn't admit it . . . But I had to track it down and be sure." Dan wiped his eyes and looked straight at O'Cleary. "So, am I right? Is this . . . this child . . . ?"

The minister said it clearly and firmly. "Dan . . . Tilly is your daughter. Your fourth child." Then he paused, considering whether to continue.

"Tell me," said Dan.

"Nine years ago Anita was there, assisting. Your daughter was from very strong stock—she was still alive after the abortion."

Dan wanted to hear the rest; he wanted to hear it all.

O'Cleary told it gently. "She . . . struggled for life for about an hour before she finally passed away in Anita's hands. Anita carried her from the clinic that day and never returned.

"It was Anita's desire that this . . . little girl . . . be given a Christian burial, so . . . I performed the services and helped meet some of the expenses.

"Every spring now, on the anniversary of the child's death, Anita goes to the grave, places flowers there, and mourns. She explained it to me once. To use her words, 'If not me, who will mourn for Tilly? Who will care to remember her?'"

Ten

Kathy and Tilly had picked some delicious fruit to enjoy; Tilly had sung a few songs, and even told Kathy a story. They were having a wonderful time.

But now it was quiet. They were sitting on the grassy knoll in the warm, embracing light, and they were silent. Tilly was sitting in a small hollow with her back against a tree; it was a perfect easy chair, probably made just for a little girl like her. Kathy was perfectly comfortable in the soft grass, and all she could do, minute upon minute, was gaze at that child. Neither of them said a word.

Maybe it's because there just aren't any safe, easy subjects left, Kathy thought.

Little girl, do you feel what I feel right now? What's going on in that little heart of yours? If only you'd say something, if only I knew what you were thinking, what you were really feeling. Tilly . . . don't close me out.

"Tilly . . ."

The brown eyes looked her way eagerly.

I've started, Kathy thought, I've got to go ahead, I've got to see it through.

"Um . . ." Oh, how do I say this? "I wonder if maybe there are some things we've both been afraid to say. I mean, I've been afraid that there are some things that you don't want to talk about . . . But then maybe *you've* been afraid that there are some things that I don't want to talk about." Tilly was listening. She seemed to understand. "Well, what I'm trying to say is . . . if it's all right with you, it's all right with me. I *want* to talk about those things." Come on, Tilly, say you agree. "Sweetheart, I don't know how long we'll be together like this. What if we never get the chance to say what we're really thinking?"

Tilly sat up straight. "I think that would be awful, Mrs. Ross."

"We need to have a serious talk. Do you think we could do that?"

"Uh-huh."

"Tilly . . . you do have a mother . . . somewhere."

"Yes, ma'am. I do."

"And someday . . . you are going to see her again. Jesus told you that."

"And I want to, Mrs. Ross. I want to very much."

Kathy sighed deeply just to calm down. "You do want to see her?"

"Yes."

"But . . . how do you think you'll feel? Do you think you might be angry with her? Do you think you might be bitter because she sent you here without even giving you a name?"

Tilly seemed concerned for Kathy's feelings. "But, Mrs. Ross, I don't hurt anymore. I love my mother."

"You love her? And you're not angry with her?"

Tilly smiled, and her face was full of peace. "I just want to see her. I think about it all the time."

"You do? What do you think about?"

Tilly looked into space, imagining the moment. "Seeing her face. Mrs. Ross, when I see her face, I'm just going to look at it and look at it and not stop until I know it and can never forget it. And I'll rest in her lap, too; I've always wanted to do that." Tilly rose from her place and leaned against the tree, caught up in her thought. "And then . . . then we could go for walks, and I'd show her all my favorite places . . . and then she could explain things to me, just her, so I'll always remember that I learned them from my mother. My very own *mother*!

"And you know what else? Maybe she could sew a dress for me, and stitch it here and there until it fit just right, and comb my hair, and show me how to wear flowers, and how to skip . . . and maybe teach me some more songs, the songs she used to sing when she was little."

Tilly drifted a little closer. "And I'd tell her that she could still hold me. I wouldn't be hurting anymore with her here, but I'd still like her to hold me close. I'd still like her to put a warm quilt on my bed, and tuck me in, and tell me her very own stories. And then we could pray together, just like we've always wanted."

Tilly dropped her eyes and fingered the folds of her dress. "That would be really nice. I still cry sometimes, just when I'm by myself, and I always wonder what it would be like to hear her soft footsteps in the hall and know she was there listening, and coming to comfort me. And I've always wondered . . ."

Her voice broke, and her big eyes watered with a deep sorrow. "I've always wondered what she would have named me. I've always wanted to have my very own name, the one that came from her, from her heart."

Kathy didn't want to upset her. She tried to keep her own tears back; she tried not to weep.

Tilly raised her head high, her little fists clenched in front of her, looked up at the trees through tear-filled eyes, and pleaded, "Oh . . . Mommy . . . will you please . . . want me? Will you take me and let me stay with you? I've always loved you, and if I could just have you with me now, I wouldn't long for anything else.

You're my mother. That's all I know. It's all I under-stand, and . . . it's all I want."

"Oh, Tilly!" It was a cry that burst from Kathy's soul, reaching for that child. "Tilly . . ." She couldn't speak through her quaking emotion. She couldn't see through her tears. "I just don't know how I'm ever going to say this . . ."

Tilly was facing her. Directly. The brown eyes met her own. There was a soul in those eyes, a longing spirit reaching out.

"Mommy . . ." The little girl called, and Kathy's heart jumped. "Would you please . . . hold me?"

Kathy's arms opened; they would hear no more thoughts or debates, no more hesitations or doubts. They opened wide, baring her heart, baring her soul.

And Tilly was there.

I'm holding a child in my arms. A real child. My child.

Accept it, Kathy. Believe it. Just believe it.

Kathy felt the soft muslin under her hands and the black hair against her cheek.

"Tilly . . . ," she spoke so softly, "Precious . . . I'm sorry . . . I'm just so sorry . . ."

Tilly's cheeks were wet against her own. Kathy could hear the sweet little voice whispering near her ear, "Don't cry, Mommy. It's all right. It's all right."

"Forgive me . . . please . . ."

"I forgive you."

"Forgive me."

"I forgive you, Mommy. I love you. Don't cry."

Forgiven. Forgiven. A poisonous, goading spear withdrew from Kathy's soul. She could feel it go; she almost collapsed from the release, and clung to Tilly to keep from falling.

My child. My child.

Slowly, unexpectedly, there came a trembling, a surrendering, and finally, of its own strength and will, a cry from deep within her that would not be held back. With another breath it became a wail, a building, gushing flood of anguish, sorrow, and remorse, all pouring forth together, draining from her heart. The flood became a lament, long and loud, flowing from Kathy's soul like a song all its own, the melody rising and falling with the anguish of her heart. The song grew, weaving strain upon strain into a long crescendo as the forest sang a quiet harmony in its own wistful sighs.

Only the forest could hear her; gently, it received her cries and carried them far away on the breeze. Nothing broke this moment; no sense of time hurried her. She was free to cry, to rock gently with this little girl in her arms as the forest embraced them, the soft light soothed them, and the creek sang reassurance. Peace was here, enough to cover and protect them, until Kathy's heart was free.

So very much later, having spent itself in tears, in cleansing, in restoration, the lament began to resolve, to settle and merge quietly with the other sounds in the forest. Kathy's head sank and her body relaxed. Tilly stirred just a little. Kathy relaxed her embrace for the first time and could feel her arms aching.

She could barely speak. "Oh, Tilly . . . I can't believe I'm even holding you. I didn't think you'd ever let me hold you."

"I never knew if you wanted to."

"Oh, I do. I really do."

Tilly kept her little arms around Kathy's neck. "Don't let go. I've never been held by my own mother before."

Kathy gave her another hug to reassure her. "Tilly, how long did you know?"

Tilly leaned back from the embrace just enough to look into her mother's eyes, her face full of wonder and delight. "I guess . . . I guess I always knew it was you. The first time I saw you, I just knew you were my mommy!"

"So . . . is that why you were crying?"

"I couldn't help it, Mommy. I just couldn't help it. I was really seeing you. I always wondered what you really looked like. All I could ever remember was the sound of your voice."

Kathy's eyes flooded again.

Tilly touched her face. "Are you happy, Mommy?"

Kathy nodded and blinked away the tears. "Oh, yes, Tilly. I'm very happy."

"I am too."

"I've just missed you so much. Even when I tried not to think about it, in my heart I always missed you."

"And I've always missed you."

"And then . . . when you told me your name . . . Tilly, deep down in my heart, for nine years, I've known you by that name. That *is* your name."

Tilly was so glad to hear that. "And I'll keep it. Thank you, Mommy."

Kathy pulled her into a close embrace once again. "Oh, you're welcome . . . Tilly."

They remained together there on the grassy knoll, with no other plans for the time being. They would be there a long while.

Eleven

$\mathcal{D}$an stood on the front porch of the little bungalow, nervously rechecking his suitcoat and tie. Out on the avenue, late-afternoon traffic roared homeward. Pastor O'Cleary lightly knocked on the door, and immediately the door opened.

Well, there she stood. After nine years Dan still knew her face.

"Hello, Pastor," she said.

O'Cleary looked at Dan. "Anita Mendoza, I'd like you to meet Dan Ross."

She offered her hand. "Hello, Mr. Ross."

He took her hand in both of his and looked into her deep brown eyes, her soft, compassionate face. "I'm very honored. Thank you for letting us drop by."

She opened her door widely. "Won't you come in?"

Twelve

*S*omewhere back in the trees, running along an unseen path through the berry vines and flowers, a mother and her giddy, giggling daughter shouted and laughed, playing together as if they'd always done it, as if it was the most natural thing in the world.

"Come on, you sing it!" came Kathy's challenge.

"All right, but you have to sing too!" said Tilly teasingly.

"Oh . . ." said Kathy, trying to catch her breath. "Let's see, where do we start it?"

Tilly proposed a starting note. "Playyyy . . ."

Kathy picked it up and the song began, a happy bouncing, teasing duet by these two unseen denizens of the forest.

> *"Playmate, come out and play with me,*
> *And bring your dollies three.*
> *Climb up my apple tree.*
> *Holler down my rainbarrel,*

Slide down my cellar door,
And we'll be jolly friends
Forevermore!"

Then Tilly shouted, "I'll race you to that tree!"

"Oh," Kathy moaned, "you're going to wear me out!"

The bushes shook, the grass swished, their footsteps pattered and thumped . . .

And here they came, bounding over a hill and down, neck and neck, Tilly's little arms like a windmill and Kathy just trying to stay on her feet.

"Hey, not so fast!" Kathy protested laughingly.

All Tilly could do was squeal.

Tilly reached the tree first, whipped around it, and then rolled into the grass, disappearing in the tall blades except for her tumbling arms and feet. Kathy reached the tree and was glad the race was over. She held on to the tree, huffing and puffing, but all smiles.

Tilly's head popped up out of the grass. "You run very well, Mommy!"

Kathy was tickled at the sight. "Well, now you know where you got those nimble legs of yours!"

Then she thought of the flowers, those laughing, nodding, bobbing flowers all around them, myriads upon myriads, and the deepest, most beautiful purple she'd ever seen.

"Oh . . ." she said as an idea occurred to her. "All right, I know I can't pass this up."

Tilly was curious. "What?"

Kathy started gathering various blooms, looking carefully for just the right ones. "Here. I want to show you how to put these flowers in your hair."

Tilly was wide-eyed with excitement. "Are you going to make me pretty, Mommy?"

"You're already pretty, sweetheart. Here, sit down."

Tilly found a handy stone to perch on, and sat down with her head forward, her back straight. She was ready.

Kathy took a comb from her pocket and started exploring the possibilities in Tilly's long tresses.

"I've been looking forward to this."

Tilly wiggled with excitement. "I've never done this before."

"Well, hold still now. Boy, you have thick hair! You're just like your father."

"Does Amy put flowers in her hair?"

"Mm, yes, especially in the springtime. But she's done a lot of different things with it."

"Well, when you come back, we can all be together and teach each other all kinds of things."

Kathy let that thought go by. All she wanted to do was comb her daughter's hair. "Let's comb it over this way. I want to see your rosy cheeks."

"I can't wait to see Amy and learn all about how she paints."

"Well, that will happen when it happens . . . What matters is that we're together now."

"Uh-huh. I just wish you could stay longer."

Tilly, don't tamper with my dream! "Sweetheart, we really don't have to talk about that now."

Tilly tried to turn her head. "Mommy . . . we have to."

Kathy ignored her. "Hold still. I'm creating a masterpiece!"

Tilly sat still as Kathy placed the flowers in her hair. Tilly and the flowers were made for each other.

But Tilly was insistent. "Mommy, I have to tell you something."

"What is it?"

Tilly said something. Kathy caught a few words, but not all of them. Another sound had intruded, another voice.

"Tilly, what did you say?"

"Mommy, please don't ever feel bad again. Remember that Jesus—"

The other voice spoke again, muffling Tilly's words. "Kathy," it said.

Kathy winced and shook her head just a little. It was troubling, irritating. "Tilly, I'm sorry, I didn't hear you."

Tilly spoke in earnest. "Jesus forgave you a long time ago, and you need to know that. Please don't feel bad anymore."

Kathy looked into those beautiful eyes. "Tilly, you know that means everything to me."

That voice again! "Kathy . . . sweetheart . . ." It was Dan! Dan was calling her!

Kathy clapped her hands over her ears. "Oh, stop it! Don't!"

Tilly was desperate. She had to get some things said, she had to make her mother listen. "Mommy . . . listen! Look at me!"

Tilly's voice sounded so muffled; Kathy could see her daughter, but . . . "Talk louder, Tilly! I can't hear you!"

The little hands reached toward her. Kathy reached to take them in her own, but they were so far away. She was groping for them.

"Mommy," she said, "always remember that I love you."

Dan called again. "Kathy, wake up . . ."

Kathy reached, almost plunging forward. She found the little hands and held them tightly. "Take my hands, Tilly! Don't let go!"

The flowers in the meadow were excited. They waved back and forth frantically. Look out, they seemed to be saying, look out, something's going to happen! A cold wind was blowing, roaring through the tops of the trees.

Tilly clung ever so tightly to her mother's hands. "And always remember that I don't hurt anymore."

Kathy found herself shouting, afraid the little child would not hear her. "You don't hurt . . . Are you sure?"

Tilly's voice sounded like it was on the other side of a thick window. The light all around her was fading into the ominous gray of an approaching storm. The wind was stirring the forest, bringing trouble, noise, confusion.

"I don't hurt at all!" came Tilly's voice. "I'm happy here!"

Dan's voice seemed to come from the sky like distant thunder. "Kathy . . . Time to wake up!"

She looked toward the stormy sky and cried into the wind, "No! No! I don't want to leave!"

Tilly tugged at her hands, imploring her in a little voice that sounded so far away. "You have to, Mommy. Bruce and Amy and Tommy and Daddy . . . they all need you. Mommy, I can't be with you now, but I'll be all right. I'll wait for you. I love you, Mommy. I love all of you."

Dan was so close now. "Kathy . . . Come on, sweetheart, wake up."

Kathy sheltered her eyes with her hands and

peered at Tilly. The image of her little child was with-drawing, fading back into a greasy, smearing fog. Oh please, Lord, let me see her one more time.

"Let me see your face, Tilly! Let me see how the flowers look!"

There she was, far away, but smiling, waving, her hair just the way Kathy had combed it, the flowers bright and perfect.

Tilly called from across the ever-widening chasm, "Life isn't that long. You'll see me. I'll let you hold me for as long as you want, and you'll never have to cry again!"

"You look beautiful!"

"I'll always keep these flowers, Mommy!"

Was it the clouds covering her fading dream, or was it the tears in her eyes that blurred her final vision of her little daughter? That precious sight was almost gone now. The distance was swallowing it up.

"Smile big for me! Let me see you!"

There was that smile again. A little hand waved. A distant, melodic voice called, "I love you, Mommy! I love you!"

Kathy could feel a hand on her shoulder, the warmth of blankets, the smells of a familiar bedroom. She heard one more very faint "I love you," and then a voice that was more real, more present.

"Kathy . . ."

She jolted awake with a gasp. Light flooded her eyes. Information registered in her mind. The ceiling. The bed. Dan.

She bolted upright. The dream was fading. It would not stay. Her eyes told her merciless truths: the wondrous light was gone from the windows . . . the backyard was silent . . . the clock was there, dutifully reminding her of how late in the day it was. Her husband, her loving husband, was there beside her, his hand calming her, his voice comforting her.

Dream, please stay. Don't be a dream. Be a part of me forever. Live in my mind, be real in my heart. Don't leave me.

But slowly, deliberately it departed, and she was awake. She began to cry.

"Hey, Kathy," Dan said softly, "it's all right. It's just me. You're okay. You're right here in your own bedroom. It's all right."

She tried to stop crying. She looked around the room just to make sure everything was as real as it seemed. It was.

"Well . . ." she admitted at last, "I guess we all have to wake up sometime, don't we?"

"Why are you crying?"

Kathy could still feel the pain of loss in her heart. That was real enough. "I was having a dream. That's all."

"You've been sleeping all day. It must have been some kind of dream."

"Oh . . . it was nothing . . ." No, Kathy was different now. *Things* were going to be different. "No! It was more than that! Dan, I want to tell you about it. We need to talk—"

"We will. We will. I promise."

"No. Right now."

Dan leaned forward and held up his hand to ease her out of bed. "There's somebody here. She wants to see you."

The very idea seemed outlandish. "Dan, look at me! I can't see anybody!"

He only smiled. "Take your time. It'll be worth it, I promise."

Thirteen

On their way down the hall toward the living room, Dan held Kathy close and only had time to say one sentence.

"After this we'll take some time, and we'll talk."

Kathy believed him. Something had changed while she was asleep.

They came into the living room, and for just a moment the dream was with her again. She could sense it, feel it, remember it.

It had to be this woman now rising from the sofa to greet her. Was she real? That moment in the cemetery could have been part of the dream, but . . . no. This was that woman, smiling timidly, extending her hand.

"Mrs. Ross?"

Kathy took the woman's hand in both of hers and looked into those dark Latin eyes. I know you. The dream was real, for me. It's still mine.

Anita Mendoza asked, "Do you remember me?"

Kathy held her hand tightly. "Why . . . why did you name her . . . Tilly?"

Anita smiled shyly. "Well . . . she . . . she just looked like a Tilly."

Fourteen

It was a day in April. A same old spring.

It could have been another funeral, this small cluster of people standing alone in the vast green expanse of the old cemetery. But it was a reunion.

Dan was there, holding Kathy close, and feeling closer to her than he'd ever been. Bruce was there; he wouldn't have missed it for the world. Amy couldn't hold back her tears of joy—she'd finally met her real mother again. Tommy didn't understand it all, but he paid attention; someday it would really mean something.

Anita was there, her time of mourning now over. She had shown them to the grave and soon, with a kiss and a blessing, she would leave them alone.

And Kathy would remain there a long while, sitting on the soft grass, recalling those big brown eyes, that playful giggle, and those loving little arms. She would think of those special moments beside the laughing creek, and sometimes she would see those tall, sheltering trees again; with just the right breeze, the smell of those faraway purple flowers would come back to her.

And she would weep quietly, with this and with every new April, for all the children who had no names and no parents, who still lived though never born.

Most of all, she would weep for the little daughter she never knew, and give whispered words to what she had always known: "Tilly, I love you."

But now her heart was at peace, and that peace was hers to keep. She only wanted to remember.

Just remember.

Other Crossway Products by
Frank E. Peretti

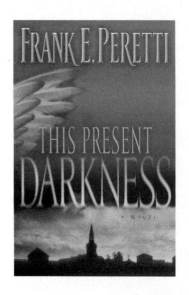

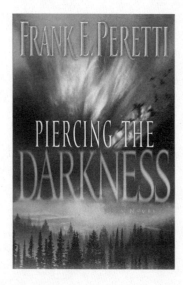